Madevhe is coming

written by [illegible]

illustrated by Lois Neethling

Translated from the original Tshivenda
[illegible]

[illegible] PUBLISHERS

Gondo was born crippled in his right leg.

He went to visit his aunt at Mananga when schools closed for the holidays. He liked to look after cattle in the veld with the other boys.

A baboon called Madevhe lived in mountains near the village. He was a very big baboon. He had very big eyes. He had very big ears. His face was very ugly. When you looked at him, your blood ran cold.

When he shouted, "Hoom! Hoom!" the sound echoed through the mountains. There was no other baboon like him in those mountains.

On the first day of the holidays Gondo went to the veld with the other boys. He did not know anything about Madevhe. Madevhe always used the same path down the mountain. The boys called Gondo to play with them on Madevhe's path.

The time came for Madevhe to come down from the mountain. Gondo played happily with his back to the mountain.

Suddenly, Madevhe appeared in the distance. The boys saw him and said quietly to each other, "Madevhe is coming. Do not tell the visitor."

So none of the boys told Gondo about the danger that was coming closer.

Suddenly all the boys shouted like a choir, "Madevhe! Madevhe!" Gondo was confused. Then he saw the baboon!

Gondo jumped up and started to run.
“I am going to die!” he screamed.

Madevhe came very close to Gondo's heels. Gondo's crippled leg made it difficult for him to run well.

Gondo limped twice and thrice. Suddenly on the fourth limp his legs began to work. He ran like a thrown object to save his dear life from Madevhe. What happened that day was a real miracle!

THE END

Thanks

We thank the following people for their help in evaluating the original *Tshivenda* version of this story:

Johana Ratshikhopha, Ndivhaleni Ramudzuli, Mashudu Ramavhunga, Violet Ratshikhopha, Leah Phuluwa, Nodia Sidogi and Tshinakaho Musie from Ralson Tshinaṋe Adult Centre, Ngovhela, Sibasa.

We thank the following people for their help in evaluating the English version of this story:

Shelley Seid (facilitator), Emily Dladla, Constance Mthembu, Dudu Laza, Armstrong Nkomo, Jabulile Sibisi and Xoliswa Hulley from the University of Natal Adult Literacy Programme.

Silas Nndwakhulu Siṱholimela

Silas Nndwakhulu Siṱholimela was born in the Nzhelele Valley. He has worked for the Venda Agricultural Corporation and the Venda Education Scheme. He is currently Vice Rector of the Madzivhandila College of Agriculture in Limpopo Province.

NEW READERS PUBLISHERS

New Readers Publishers is a non-profit publishing project based in the School of Community Development and Adult Learning at the University of Natal in Durban. The aim of the project is to contribute to an increase in adult literacy and the promotion of a reading culture. It does this by developing and publishing easy readers in all of South Africa's official languages and by increasing the capacity of teachers through training. The books are read for education and entertainment in first or additional languages.

New Readers Publishers is supported by Rockefeller Brothers Fund.

How to contact us

If you want to find out more about New Readers Publishers or about other books that we publish, please contact:

New Readers Publishers
School of Community Development and Adult Learning
University of Natal
Durban
4041

Tel: 031 – 2602568
Fax: 031 – 2601168
E-mail: keyser@nu.ac.za
Website: www.nrp.und.ac.za

Madevhe is coming

English version first published 2002 by
New Readers Publishers
School of Community Development and Adult Learning
University of Natal, Durban 4041
South Africa

Translated from **Mirubo ya vhatukana** (*Tshivenda*)

Cover illustration by Lois Neethling
Design and desktop publication by Lesley Lewis of Inkspots, Durban
Printed by Interpak Books, Pietermaritzburg

ISBN: 1-86840-478-1